Raven's Resilience

Friendly High School Students

Illustrated by

G David Cooper

2021-2022 Friendly High School Freshmen students collaborated in the writing of this writing project sponsored by The Better Place, Inc. Student Contributors include: Zora Ashaka, Dakotah Anderson, Jasmine Bautista, Dominique Combs, Valerie Galeasmoreira, Bailey Green, Emmalee Harris, Jaiden Johnson, Yaneli Mendozamejia, Damia Moore, Gerahmae Petarte, Nazir Rodriguez, Sabrina Santossalvarado, Makailah Smoot, Aissata Sylla, Leopole Tandjong, Ximena Venturaescobar, Samuel Villatoro, Lola Watso, Nazir Rodriguez, Jayden Morris, Daphne Bruner, Raven Jackson, Sydney Stewart, Zaria Oliver Summary on the back of book should be: Raven has a repeated pattern of rough days at school. With help from her friends and big sister, see how she chooses to respond to the situations and what she learns from it.

Printed in the United States of America

ISBN: 978-1-957443-07-2

First Printing, 2023

JayMedia Publishing

Laurel, MD 20708

www.publishing.jaymediagroup.net

Raven!

This morning my sister Caydence woke me up.
I started the morning by brushing my teeth and
eating breakfast. After that I put my clothes on and
raced out of the house to catch the bus and start
my wonderful day. Once at school, I stopped at the
cafeteria to talk to some friends. Shortly after that, I
made my way to my first class.

In class, I walked around Mia's desk to get to my seat. Once in my seat, Mia and her friends surrounded me. I felt threatened and scared that they were going to hurt me. Mia's friends looked intimidating because they were taller and older than me. I watched as they looked at each other and started laughing at me. I don't know why they were laughing at me, but it really hurt my feelings.

This morning, the next school day, my sister
Caydence woke me up. I started the morning by
brushing my teeth and eating breakfast. After that,
I put my clothes on and raced out of the house to
the bus to start my wonderful day. Once at school
I stopped at the cafeteria to talk to some friends.
After that I made my way to my first class.

Da'quan is a student from Maryland who lives with his mother and father in a big luxurious house. He is pretty popular in school and gets a lot of attention from people. When I see him at school, he does not act nice. I saw him in a big group of people and I had to walk past him to get to my locker. He said, "Look at that black girl. She's ugly." He and all his friends started laughing. I walked off confused and sad.

This morning, the next school day, my sister
Caydence woke me up. I started the morning by
brushing my teeth and eating breakfast. After that
I put my clothes on and raced out of the house to
the bus to start my wonderful day. Once at school
I stopped at the cafeteria to talk to some friends.
After that I made my way to my first class.

As I walked down the hallway, Liliana looked at me and she pushed me saying "Move, dork." I sighed and walked to class. I felt worse when she pushed me. It seemed like I was her favorite target and I didn't appreciate it much. Liliana was nice to everybody else; but towards me, she used hurtful words like dork, loser, and nerd which hurt me emotionally. We used to be friends, almost like sisters. She lost interest in being friends when she transferred to middle school. I now seem to be the focus of her hatred.

I woke up again to my sister for the fourth time. I was tired of this constant replay of negative events. In class, our teacher paired students up. I was paired up with this boy named Hunter. I went to Hunter, said "Hello," and began working on our assignment. He ignored me so I decided to focus on working on the project. I tried to talk to him again but he yelled "DO YOUR PEOPLE KNOW HOW TO TAKE A HINT?" I was shocked and hurt, I should have expected this though. I wonder why these events keep on repeating...

1. Listen wh
are talkir
2. Follow di
3. Keep har
objects t
4. Work qui
not distur
5. Show res
and pers
6. Work anc
safe mar
STAY COOL
14

This morning, for another day of school, my sister Caydence woke me up. I started the morning by brushing my teeth and eating breakfast. After that, I put my clothes on and raced out of the house to the bus to start my wonderful day. Once at school I stopped at the cafeteria to talk to some friends. I decided to talk about what was happening to me with my friends in the cafeteria before class. I realized I wasn't the only one going through difficulties and it made me feel better to know I wasn't alone in what I was going through and how I was feeling.

Spanish for Beginners
CHOCOLATE MILK
16

Despite everything that went wrong, I felt better knowing I wasn't alone. I got permission to talk to my school counselor, realizing how talking helped me feel better. When I got home, I decided to talk with my sister Caydence and the positive energy I felt from talking out what I was experiencing, feeling, and thinking felt like a breath of fresh air. Caydence encouraged me to begin using a journal and that made me feel good too. Inside I felt like a huge anvil was being lifted off of my heart and my mind. I never realized how much talking out your problems and writing about your thoughts and feelings could make a difference in how you feel, even when your problems don't go away. I feel like I can better face my challenges at school knowing I have people to talk to and activities I can use to help me feel better.

The End